N. GLOUCESTER

That's Hockey

For my little girl, Victoria: You can do better than making the Montreal Canadiens, sweetheart. You can make the Canadian Women's Olympic Team! And for the best Canadiens fan anywhere: For you, Papa.

DAVID BOUCHARD

One Sean to rule them all, One Sean to find them, One Sean to bring them all, and with karaoke, Simard them.

DEAN GRIFFITHS

That's Hockey

written by David Bouchard
illustrated by Dean Griffiths

ORCA BOOK PUBLISHERS

"Put it in gear," Etienne said. "The game starts in half an hour."

"I'm there, ET," I said, perking up. I was spending the weekend with my cousin on the farm, two whole days of hockey.

Etienne and I lived for hockey.

"What's all this?" I said when he tossed me a toque and an old, ratty Montreal Canadiens sweater. "I've given away stuff twice this good! Where are our skates? Our pads and gloves?"

"That stuff's for city kids," he said. "We play real hockey here. No skates. No pads. No helmets. Just a number nine sweater. You know, like the Rocket. Come on . . . Let's go!"

We hustled down the street with our two stubby sticks.

Down around the corner, a bunch of kids were feverishly at work clearing the road. Snow was everywhere. It must have been ten feet deep in spots.

"What's happening?" I asked.

"Clearing the ground," ET answered. "Hockey's not meant to be played indoors, you know. You'll get the hang of it. Come on!"

A couple of kids were rooting around in the ditch and in the pile of coats by the side of the road.

"What are they looking for?" I asked.

"Goal posts," my cousin answered. "Did you think we used that net in our garage? We don't. We improvise. We're looking for big chunks of hard snow, or fair-sized rocks. See? Moose's got a good chunk. We'll use that, Bennie's boots and Ben's jacket. Perfect! It's done.

"And no, we don't use a puck either. Pucks don't slide on the road and they hurt like crazy. Tooth usually brings an old red ball . . . He's got it. We're all set!"

Everyone huddled together.
"What's happening now?" I whispered.

"We're picking teams. Don't worry. This is easy. Hey, guys! I brought my cousin along. You all okay with that? Right, you're in. If you don't get picked, just follow me. You'll be on my team. Oh, and Mop ALWAYS gets picked first. Mop's that big guy."

And was he ever big! He looked like somebody's dad in kid's clothes.

A few kids waved their arms around and everyone started shuffling to one end or the other.

"This is picking teams?" I asked.

"Well, yeah. Teams kind of just happen. Come on. You're with us."

I was getting frustrated. Was this a hockey game or some secret ritual?

When we got to our end, ET told me more. "See that kid over there. What do you notice about him?"

"No front teeth."

"Right. He had them knocked out twice last year and his dad won't get him new ones till he quits playing hockey. We call him Tooth. He plays goal. Always."

We were ready to play.

The ball hit the road and the game was on.

Once the game started, time stopped for me. For all of us.

We played. And played. And played.

And were they good! I never saw a pro handle a puck the way these kids handled an old red ball. Mop, the only one who had a chance of making the NHL, stood in one spot grabbing, knocking, tripping or elbowing anyone within reach.

I didn't touch the ball until much later, when it appeared on my stick and the road opened up before my eyes.

I was alone on goal. Me against Tooth. I raced forward and in one move faked left and shot right. Tooth went down and I fired the ball over his left shoulder.

I scored!

I jumped for the sky and ET hollered, "Hey! You guys see that? Does my cousin have moves or what?"

He turned toward me. "Is this the best?" he screamed.

It was the best, even when it turned out that I had just been part of another grand tradition of the game: everybody scores.

I didn't care. It was awesome!

We played on for hours, maybe days. Who knew?

I scored a pack of goals. Everybody did. Even the goalies broke with the puck now and then and scored. The game went on and on and on.

Then Tooth yelled out, "Next goal wins!"

The game was ending. Win or lose, it came down to that last goal.

So I thought.

I played my heart out. We had to win. I ran faster than I had ever run before. I checked everyone in sight, even Mop! I threw my body in front of a blazing shot, but it was no use. The ball was in. They had scored and we had lost.

Or had we?

As I turned to see how ET would take defeat, Mop yelled, "Next goal wins," and the game went on.

Another goal. Another call for victory. Another. And another.

How it ended, who left first, I don't know. The ball was still in play when I noticed that the teams had shrunk.

One goal post disappeared, then two.

Etienne gave the nod. We headed home.

"My toes are numb!" he said as we stepped into the house. "Sit here by the stove. Put your feet up and get ready for the last tradition of street hockey."

His mom had something waiting for us.

"Every game finishes with hot chocolate," my cousin said.

We sat in the kitchen talking about shots and saves, the NHL, our next game, our dreams.

"You know," ET said finally, "I didn't have any money to buy you a Christmas present. But you can keep my sweater. It worked real well for you today!"

For years, ET's sweater worked for me. And now it's time to pass it on to you.

    "But Mom, I've never played street hockey."

"With this sweater, sweetheart, you'll do just fine."

National Library of Canada Cataloguing in Publication Data
Bouchard, Dave, 1952-
That's hockey

ISBN 1-55143-223-4

1. Hockey–Juvenile literature. I. Title

GV847.25.B67 2002   j796.962   C2002-910364-9

First published in the United States, 2002

Library of Congress Control Number: 2002103670

Summary: Etienne introduces his city cousin to the joys and eccentricities of real hockey, street hockey that is.

Teacher's guide available from Orca Book Publishers.

Orca Book Publishers gratefully acknowledges the support of its publishing programs provided by the following agencies: the Department of Canadian Heritage, the Canada Council for the Arts, and the British Columbia Arts Council.

Design by Christine Toller
Printed and bound in Hong Kong

IN CANADA:
Orca Book Publishers
PO Box 5626, Station B
Victoria, BC Canada
V8R 6S4

IN THE UNITED STATES:
Orca Book Publishers
PO Box 468
Custer, WA USA
98240-0468

04 03 02 • 5 4 3 2 1